EVA'S
IMAGINATION

EVA'S
IMAGINATION

WENDA SHURETY
ILLUSTRATED BY KAREN ERASMUS

Eva flung herself onto the soft carpet of the study.

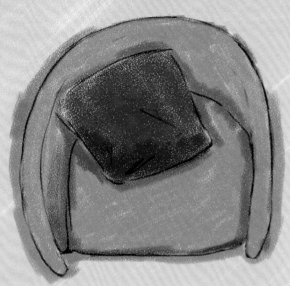

'Mum, I'm BORED!'

'What's happened to your imagination, Eva?' asked Mum.

Eva sat up. 'What's an imagination?'

'You'll know when you find it,' Mum smiled.

'Come on, Chops.
Let's hunt for my
imagination,' said Eva.

She made a list of everything
they would need.

'Snacks.'

'Good shoes.'

'A stick.'

Eva set off with Chops trotting behind.
The sun shone brightly as they made their way through the narrow valley.

After a long walk, they reached a dense forest.
Eva peered through the pine trees.
'What's that noise?'
A cuckoo called in the distance.

Moving a branch aside, Eva stepped beneath
the forest canopy.

'Let's search behind every tree.'
Eva had a good look.
Chops had a good sniff.
Nothing was there but a dirty old napkin. Or was it?

Soon the travellers were climbing up a steep mountainside.
The wind whistled past their ears.
'Let's stop for a rest,' puffed Eva.

Eva and Chops sat side by side on a
rock, eating bananas and dog biscuits.
'Are we nearly there yet?'

They tramped up the rest of the mountain as
cottonwool clouds drifted below them.
Eva could make out other mountains
in the distance.

'I think I can see a cave. That must be the place where my imagination is hiding!'

The explorers raced to the cave's entrance and stared into the dark.
Brave Eva and Chops crawled into the shadows: first their heads, then
their shoulders ... and finally they were all the way in.

Eva felt around and screamed when her hand touched something furry.
Was there a scary creature guarding the treasure?

'Snowy!' yelled Eva. 'I thought I had lost you.'
Chops sniffed Eva's favourite toy.

'Where to next?'

Eva and Chops trekked over a bridge to a rainforest on the other side.

Trees loomed over them. Every space was packed with ferns
and vines of vibrant colours.

Eva ventured in, waving her stick to create a path through the wilderness.
'Follow me, Chops!'
Something long and thin dangled in front of Eva's face.

'Snaaaaake!' she screamed.

Eva ran towards Chops, who was sniffing behind a bush.
'X marks the spot! What have you found?'
Nothing but some storybooks.

'It's no use, Chops. I can't find an imagination anywhere!'
Eva heaped the books into her backpack and made her way back down
the mountain. Mum was waiting at the bottom.

'Mum, we couldn't find my imagination,' said Eva, 'but we found Snowy and some great books. We had the best adventure together!'